THE COURAGE
TO WALK
AND
WRITE

Pria Louka

For Mr. LaMotte

ISBN 0692531467
PRINTED IN THE USA

I was walking through the woods when I heard a deer scramble and jump into the water. It galloped through the creek, sprays of light and gushing water and power, animals sleek like a wave's crest. It's always full of light there. The trickling water that reminds me of my own blood, and my quiet, wet footprints leave a mark without a sound. Or the crawfish feeding on algae underwater, brown fur ripples of deer leaping high, they fed under the light. I watched a turtle fall from its high post onto its shell. The dragonflies, blue and red. Buzzing, in the light, it is such a dream. I consider never writing about it, so that it's like a dream lost in forever. Then, one day I'll come across some scent or sight and experience such nostalgia. With writing, you lose that. You lose that nostalgia. Today, there wasn't as much light, only a silver cloud gleam. The sound of a far-away motor drilled itself into me like an echo. The reflection and the clouds disappearing into the wide expanse of dark green trees. I started to remember Chopin and realized how many sighs Chopin sighed. He had a sensitive and winding soul, it spiraled like dandelion seeds to the moon and then a gentle nymph caught them for wishes, then it would blow to another hand and spiral to another light. The left hand, I sat on the rock, his palm.

9/8/14

Contents

The Courage to Walk and Write

When I walk, I hold onto the thoughts and images I want to write about. Listening to ambulances from the woods, snowflakes that fall from gray skies and looked like they've emerged from nothing, a large tree surrounded by thorns that I lean against, a white fence continuing into a sky that is white or violet or pale yellow or even green. And when I feel like I've forgotten something, I panic and try hard to remember everything that I've seen. I was walking towards my neighborhood in the night when a number of cars sped by, lighting up the grass with their headlights, illuminating an expanse of spider webs. I felt as though I had to stop walking and watch the field as it turned ghostly white in order to truly appreciate it. But somehow I couldn't bring myself to stop. So I kept moving and the field then seemed to spread out inside of me like shadows, mobility, and dying.

To have the courage to walk and write means you aren't afraid of losing thoughts and images that come to mind. Because you know that currents dance and blend, you can always return to what you feel. Remembering can be just as present and creative as dreaming.

The courage to walk and write is the courage to let go.

I feel a strong resistance towards sharing my writing. This resistance comes from within and seems inherent to who I am. I cannot perform the pieces I love on the piano. I used to tell myself that this uncontrollable need to hold onto my feelings was a sign that I had already given enough of myself. I imagined my energy to be pressed into the tree lines of forests I liked to walk through. But with all the natural disasters, terrorist attacks, riots, and deaths that occurred this past year, I've come to feel my mortality deeply. And the only way I can cope with this feeling is to let go—I want to give my love and live for the world.

There is a vitality, a life force, an energy, a quickening that is translated through you into action, and because there is only one of you in all of time, this expression is unique. And if you block it, it will never exist through any other medium, and be lost. The world will not have it. It is not your business to determine how good it is, nor how valuable, nor how it compares with other expressions. It is your business to keep it yours, clearly and directly, to keep the channel open. You do not even have to believe in yourself or your work. You have to keep open and aware directly to the urge that motivates you. Keep the channel open.

Martha Graham to Agnes DeMille

The pieces of writing in this collection are all centered on letting go. Letting go of silence for words or songs, letting go of memories and dreams for internal vibrancy.

I hope that through sharing this collection I will be able to express my feelings of hope and love and respond compassionately to people who need to be listened to. I hope, in the future, to write and share the stories of people who never got the chance to tell the story.

5/20/15

Warrior of Liberty

Whenever I face the Cuban sun, I feel the glimmering power of his eyes. So I stand in the rays and remember.

"José, please go back to the rearguard, you are not a warrior. Anyway, you can't die, your very life represents all we are fighting for. Without you, there is no revolution," I whined and begged. We had a very small chance of winning. The rebel group had told me we were betrayed by a campesino and that the colonial troops were coming fast.

"Máximo," it was the first time he called me by my real name, "I will stand here, beside you and these men. Last night I told them to fight until death, so how can I not be alongside them? I have chosen the path of struggle and therefore, I will take it. He who gives his life to serve a great idea is admirable... to give one's life is a right only when one gives it unselfishly (Ripoll)*. My life is for Cuba."

His eyes glimmered in the afternoon sun. I cringed as I noticed how boldly his dark clothing contrasted his white horse. He was an open and easy target. Not a warrior.

"They are here! Look! *Joven, a la carga!*" José shouted ferociously.

*Words spoken by José Marti are indicated by the citation Ripoll (Ripoll, Carlos. "Martí." Free Cuba Foundation. 2008)

"General, should we go?" asked one of the men, eyeing the frail figure.

"Why ask me? Do not distrust him, he is the reason you are here today."

The men went after him, but José was far ahead. It seemed as if he alone were confronting the entire Spanish infantry.

I remember what he told me the night before. I had come up to him and said we were only four thousand men and that we would never win against the Spanish, who were at least thirteen thousand.

He looked to the sky, as he always did when thinking, and said, "One just principle from the depths of a cave is more powerful than an army, and then, like stones rolling down hills, fair ideas reach their objectives despite all obstacles and barriers. It may be possible to speed or hinder them, but impossible to stop them (Ripoll). That is how I know we will win, Señor Gómez, liberty is on our side. We are more powerful than they."

And here he was, impossible to stop. I rode towards him, faster and faster, towards liberty.

Then I heard three consecutive shots and stopped immediately, as if I were the one being shot. My eyes looked up just in time to see the National Hero himself release the reins of his horse and fall. My eyes stung with burning tears. I ran towards him and felt for his heartbeat.

"José, please, say something!"

He turned his head towards the sun, eyes wide open in silent poetry, blood draining into Cuban soil.

I looked up too. The sun warmed me, drying the tears that had already flowed out.

Then I rode fast, to catch up with the warriors, to find this new land that our hero had shown us, and to live there in his honor.

His diary—that is all I could recover. The Spanish found his body and took it as a prize. Oftentimes, when I'm alone, I take the diary and go outside to remember him. He would be so happy to see a free Cuba, but he already knew it was going to happen, he knew the stones would eventually reach the bottom of the hill. I never actually read the diary though—I just hold it and feel its leather covering. Sometimes I lift it towards the sun to see if its leather glistens like José's eyes. Then, I am reminded of the first day I met him, the day I first noticed those eyes.

I kept glancing at the clock. I sat down by the window, waiting anxiously for the arrival of my new roommate. They told me that he needed to be taken special care of. A black carriage slowly pulled up to the entrance of the dormitory. Two guards rushed in with a small, thin boy. I almost had to laugh, such a small person, what could he have done to be deported from Cuba to Spain?

I opened the door and the two guards rushed in.

"We are in a hurry, Señor Gómez, this is your new roommate, José Martí. And these are the papers"

I closed the door behind them and remember being surprised as I turned around to face José. I never saw such dark eyes, such power in such a frail figure. In those dark eyes, there was a glimmer like stars shining through overwhelming darkness.

"Hello Señor Martí, how come you've entered the University so late in the year?" I asked, pitying the eighteen-year-old boy.

"Because I love liberty. Like bones to the human body, the axle to the wheel, the wing to the bird, and the air to the wing, so is liberty the essence of life... (Ripoll)," he sighed.

While José went off to the law school the next day, I read the package of papers. José had been arrested in his homeland, Cuba, when he was fifteen for helping create an anti-colonial newspaper. He spent three years in jail, then was deported here, to the University of Zaragoza of Spain, to study law.

All he talked about was Cuba. And he was busy all the time writing, noticing, observing.

Then, one evening towards the end of the year, he asked me, "Where are you from, Señor Gómez?"

I hesitated, hoping he would not scorn my lack of patriotism, then responded cautiously, "The Dominican Republic."

He nodded his head, "So why did you join the Spanish army?"

"I needed the money... Why do you ask?"

"No reason," he responded. But as he walked out the door, I heard him murmur, "Those who have you, o Liberty, do not know you. Those who do not have you should not speak of you, but win you (Ripoll). I shall win you."

I remember the last day at Zaragoza. José was watching me pack my bags with a sort of intensity, then asked sternly, "Now that you have finished your military training here in Spain, Señor Gómez, where will you go?"

"Cuba," I said.

"Cuba? What happened there? Is there a revolt?" he asked worriedly.

"I don't know. I'm going for personal business."

"What kind?" he asked more relaxed.

"I have decided to retire from the Spanish army and join the Cuban army." I stopped packing and waited for his approval—he was the one who made me change my mind.

"Good, good, they need people like you, radicals, genuine men who see things in their depth (Ripoll)," he said with deep satisfaction, "I will be there soon, we have much to do."

That same year, I led a campaign in Guantanamo to get rid of the Spanish forces. It was so violent and so bloody, it blinds me even today. I came up with "The Machete Charge," and they all hailed me for transforming the Cuban Army ("Máximo Gómez").

There were countless times when I would question myself. Wasn't killing against liberty? I wished to talk to my young friend from Zaragoza and ask him to define liberty for me, but he wasn't there.

I didn't see José again until about twenty years later. But I knew all about him through small pieces of information.

I remember reading the newspaper one morning. It told the story of a young journalist from Mexico City escaping to Guatemala for resisting the military regime. The first sentence of the article had been a quote by this journalist: "Man loves liberty, even if he does not know that he loves it. He is driven by it and flees from where it does not exist (Ripoll)." I knew who said that even before I read the rest.

After that, I lost track of José. No one knew where he was, so I had forgotten about him until Julian Perez sent me a telegram in 1884. I did not know this "Julian Perez," but he sounded exactly like José. It was quite nauseating to feel that voice haunt me again. Julian Perez wrote to me to tell me to be patient, that it was still too early to win Cuba back. I responded and said that I disagreed, the timing was perfect to invade. And then, he wrote to me all about his work. He was raising money for the revolution and organizing trained men in New York, South America, and Jamaica through clubs. Perez wrote with such delicate, polite, familiar language, that I decided to prolong the uprising. Otherwise, I would never listen to a stranger.

Meanwhile, I heard of José again. Everyone started to know who he was now. Those speeches he gave in New York, those plays, those novels, they sprung up everywhere. Weapons and men entered everyday illegally and the army became larger and larger. We read of revolts for the Cuban Revolution in New York, and stories of support from the Spanish living in Cuba. It became big news when José resigned from his post as the Consul of Argentina in the U.S. to come to Cuba when he heard that the Home-Rule Party could not receive justice from the Spanish government. He came over to fight.

The more I read, the more I felt a tingling pain in my heart, like a frustrated kind of anger. What happened to the peaceful political revolutionary whose ideas were greater than violence? Had fame blocked his love for peace? He wasn't a warrior, it would be wrong for him to be one. I was here, in Cuba, to fight for passionate patriotic feelings. His power existed in words, not on the battlefield. The battlefield was for me.

Now, when I think back onto this anger, I am not sure where it came from. Perhaps I felt defensive because José had become a public figure when before, he was only in my knowledge, like an inner conscience. Or maybe I just wished the voice of liberty use only peace to bring peace. I am not sure, perhaps I was simply jealous.

I couldn't stop reading about him though. The more I tried to stop, the more I felt I disconnected from everything. Reading what José wrote made me resurface from dazes of restlessness and a want for escape. I remember watching dust particles dance in the rays of afternoon sun, and feeling a strong desire to let tears drown away everything I have ever done. His poetry guided me with calm principles back to the surface, every time, just before the moment of drowning.

In 1892, I heard he returned to Cuba and stayed in Key West, the heart of the Cuban exile community. People told of the elegant speeches he gave to the workers in the tobacco industry and how he united them for the revolution. He then started a newspaper called *Patria* for his newly created Cuban Revolutionary Party, which everyone read. José travelled everywhere, hero of the country, hero of New York, hero of South America, raising more and more money. Busily revolving around and around, revolving for the revolution.

I remember, a year later, I was back in the Dominican Republic and staying in Monte Cristi when I received another strange telegram. It was from an "old friend who needed to talk of serious matters."

I saw him again on a sunny June day.

"Señor Gómez, do you remember me?" he asked with a broad grin, a grin I never saw during my time with him at Zaragoza. Those powerful eyes still drilled holes into mine, but this time, they were of a different light. They held the light of sun, burning brightly in the day, not of a star trying to shine through the night.

"I know you, but I don't know if you are the one I remember," I responded grimly, "Why didn't you send me at least one telegram after all those years?"

He chuckled, "I did, seven years ago, don't you remember Julian Perez?"

"Yes, I do. Why didn't you just tell me that was you?"

"And be caught? They were after me."

"So, what are your plans now?" I asked.

"We must start the uprising, very soon. Everything is almost ready Señor Gómez."

"Yes, yes, it's all up to you. I haven't been doing much for this country recently. You are the one who knows what to do."

"But you are the Generalissimo of the Cuban Army! I will be proud to fight besides you!" he answered with a voice of trickling reassurance.

I turned to him, "Do not fight José, you are not a warrior, leave death to me and you can make life through poetry and peace. We need both for this war."

"It is my duty," he said strongly and gazed at the clear sky, "it is my duty, to serve my country, and I have come to realize that the people can only taste freedom if action is taken. Action is the dignity of greatness (Ripoll). Men of action, above all those whose actions are guided by love, live forever. Other famous men, those of much talk and few deeds, they soon evaporate... (Ripoll)"

We planned for the revolution in the Dominican Republic for the next two years. Then declared the Manifesto of Monte Cristi. The battle began where our hero died, in Dos Rios, Two Rivers.

Sometimes I visit Matanzas, the place where my son works. Matanzas, *"La Atenas de Cuba"*, the *"Athens of Cuba"*, as the poets call it. When I am alone there, I take walks in Parque Libertad, around the central bronze statue. It shows José, lifting an arm and looking down, caught in the moment of thinking before saying something grand. I just shake my head, the statue is wrong. When José thinks he looks up, not down. He looks to the sky and lets vastness reflect in his shimmering eyes.

When I am in Parque Libertad, Liberty Park, I remember the day of his death at Dos Rios and rediscover something every time.

"Men of action," he once told me, "live forever..."

Every time in Matanzas, the city of three rivers, I discover José was the warrior I never recognized.

José Martí, warrior of humanity, warrior of action, he will live forever, a bronze statue in the heart of liberty.

Lesvos

Today I'll write of disappearances or into them
Like mountains through hazy horizons,
I could not tell, heaven or earth, for love, where I was

A faded sunset reached out through olive trees
but I could not tell whether
the leaves were red by light or by birth or life

A white horse mane like weeds and whispers
through catches of olive grove, running in and out
but breathing whole, it disappeared
like speckling stars we see so clearly from mountains,
below, red rocks and islands and two sheep stare,
their bells like churches, old rocky ones
that we love more than new ones
cause they're closer to creation

Flowers dry, pink and rocky, warming icons,
Water the taste of sheep, figs, and the idea of pears
I just remembered a glimpse from last night's dream

Iphigenia

AGAMEMNON: Such stillness. I've never felt such a stillness.

NESTOR: Be assured Agamemnon, victory does lie ahead. Do you see how our torches glimmer, casting great shadows upon Troy? It is you who will charge Troy's walls—walls built by the gods themselves. Why are you so quiet? Why do your eyes turn pleadingly towards the moon? Is there anything sweeter in life than glory?

AGAMEMNON: Nestor, you were not there in Aulis when it all happened. None of the men dare speak a word of it because it was so shameful, it leaves me sleepless every night. My wife Clytemnestra, I last remember her staring into the ocean, at our thousand ships. Her hair tangled, her eyes wild. She watched us from the topmost peak. As we sailed off towards the horizon, I could make out her silhouette disappearing amongst the shades of mountain, the crevice below. She might have killed herself Nestor. But why should I care? She's too far away. I felt myself fade into far distance, the waves crashed against the hull. I swear she cursed us. That's why we've been here for ten years and victory's yet to come. It's all my fault.

NESTOR: Just tell me what happened. It's wrong to harbor it so deep inside you.

AGAMEMNON: But I was not myself. The gods blinded me with a divine madness. I can't explain it to you.

NESTOR: Trust me, I've seen many things.

AGAMEMNON: As she walked up to the altar Nestor, my own daughter Iphigenia, I could not move my legs though I desperately wanted to run and hold her close. As she passed me, she paused and looked right through me. Her eyes glinted like the far ocean, near horizon, at the brink of reality, borderline of heaven... Just an hour earlier, she had grasped my knees begging, "Father, why would I ever want to die? All I want is to walk under the sun's light. Better to be unhappy and alive than dead and glorified!" O Iphigenia, how wrong you were... Nestor, when the smoke rose from the altar, the man who sacrificed her looked straight at me and my stance was suddenly a thousand times weaker, my skin felt as though it had been peeled back, my limbs and blood stinging and burning. I screamed so loud but the sound was drowned out by the thousand screams behind me. Screams of joy, celebratory screams. The armies were cheering for the sacrifice of my daughter. And my own scream only added to their wild din and savage joy. As they ran towards the ships, I ran up the altar. The faster I ran, the more the wind blew. When I reached the top, I could barely move because the wind was so strong. I tried to feel for my daughter's body, but it wasn't there. When I turned back, I saw that most of the men were already sailing for Troy. All was stillness, as it is now. Except for the wind rushing past me. And I found my daughter's bridal veil caught on a hanging cliff, its fabric waving to the wind... Yes, my daughter wanted to wear a bridal gown to her sacrifice. She had said, "Death is my marriage, my child, my eternal glory." And she was so young.

NESTOR: Iphigenia, sacrificed? But I was told she died of sickness. How did this happen? Why did she have to die that way?

AGAMEMNON: I ask myself that same question every night. I ask the gods—if gods even exist—why, why, why. I haven't even told you the oracle yet. Calchas shared it only with me and Menelaus: "To Artemis, the goddess guardian of the sacred forest of Aulis desecrated by the Greeks with blood, Agamemnon must sacrifice his eldest daughter Iphigenia. If he accepts, the wind will blow, and the ships will sail and the Greeks will defeat Troy. Or else, they will never leave." I was sweating. My own clothes chilled me when I stepped outside, though it was boiling even more out there. And then I saw thousands of torches descending into the valley. All of our men, all of Greece, chanting. They came to my doorstep. Over a thousand men Nestor! And the heat simmered in swarming waves. Menelaus whispered into my ear, "They're waiting for you to speak. Speak, speak, speak!" I opened my mouth and all of Greece fell silent, "The oracle says we must make a sacrifice... " I hesitated there... but all of Greece picked up on my words and began to chant, "Sacrifice, sacrifice, sacrifice!" Throughout the night the armies chanted. It was to their rhythm that I wrote that cursed letter. As the moon rose, Artemis full and pure, reigning and heading a rising chant, I imagined my daughter in a long white robe. It was as though she weren't my own anymore, a wavering shade, so far away in my mind. I didn't even stop to remember her face or her smile, or what her name meant to me. It never even struck me, that night, that Iphigenia was my own blood. I'll tell you what I wrote in the letter only if you promise me you'll not abandon me for Achilles. You already know he hates me. If I lose you to him I don't know what I'll do.

NESTOR: It is by divine law that I obey you, King.

AGAMEMNON: I wrote a letter to Iphigenia, and her mother in Argos, to come to our camp in Aulis so that she may marry Achilles. *Achilles* was the bait I used to lure them. I didn't even ask him if I could use his name. I told Iphigenia to come to Aulis by the next full moon. I guess a part of me still held back. I remember thinking: so many days, it cannot be that in so many days the wind does not blow. All my hopes. After that one night, Nestor, that one letter, everything was out of my control.

NESTOR: But why didn't you send a messenger to stop them from coming?

AGAMEMNON: I did not know what I wanted. And I hid behind such a rage. All those men who loved me and admired me, I shut my door on them, trying to isolate myself, trying to make myself believe that sacrificing my own daughter was natural as it *was* god's word. But I felt strongly, Nestor, that it was an unnatural act and repeated several times over, "It won't happen. I'll stop it." All of a sudden, I stopped chanting and waited for something. All was still, not a single breath or breeze. The shapes around me were all quiet and simple. The barrel of wine, how its simple shape emerged from the shadows was almost calming. And then her voice rang, so clear, "Father! Father! We're here!"

You know what my prayer has been these past thousand nights, Nestor? *Everything will be done as fate desires. Fate rules, not me. There's never a way to turn back.* That is my comfort.

I ran to the door as soon as I heard her voice. If a stranger had been observing me they'd think it a loving moment—a father rushing to greet his daughter. But all I could think was, "Since evil must happen, let it happen immediately." I guess I longed to see her too though... She put her arms around my neck and sighed, "Oh I've missed you so much." And I cried hard in her embrace. You can't cry so hard unless you truly love someone, right?

I don't know how Clytemnestra found out about the oracle. But when she did, she looked nobler than ever before, a real queen. "Let me ask you something," she said, "and if you are a man, you will answer: are you going to kill our daughter?"

I couldn't even look her in the eye. And she screamed and took me by my shoulders and tried to bring me down. I did the same to her, screaming, "I can't, I can't do anything! This cannot be undone." After that moment, Nestor, I lost everything. Even if Iphigenia had not been sacrificed, I would never be able to face her again, knowing what I could have done. And the love Clytemnestra had always felt for me would be dead. I'd return home from bloody war to murderous glares and murdering shame. After Clytemnestra learned the truth, nothing, nothing could be undone. I ran out the door into the sacred forest of Aulis and waited for the time of the sacrifice. A deer with golden antlers made her way through the olive grove, fur rippling for every breath, she wandered through spots of sunlight. As the deer galloped away, my daughter emerged into view, gasping and shuddering. I could tell she had already found out she was going to be sacrificed. She bit her lip and fell to her knees. After a while, she lay back and looked up to the sky and whispered something. From a grove, I watched my daughter sigh alone. But Menelaus' party found her just in time for the sacrifice. She had nowhere to escape. And I was too ashamed to face her. But here we are now, ten years later, and tens of thousands have died. It's like my daughter died for death.

NESTOR: How can you say that? You'll never know what she died for. Just before the sacrifice, her eyes glinted like the far ocean, near horizon, brink of reality, borderline of heaven. A deer with golden antlers mingled in her presence as she prayed to the light. It's as though your daughter died for life.

Newborn Pain

The storm just subsided and it looks as though a fire went out. Clouds are heavenly, breathing through a deep blue-purple, the dangerous color of thunder. Branches frame a patch of sky and I imagine an embryo in all its newborn pain rotating inside that frame. I was listening to the music of Russian villagers that dance in circles around a birch tree, a fantasy land for only prayers and begging royally.

It's been a year since my great uncle died. I wonder if I'm the only one who remembers. My grandmother didn't mention anything on the phone, but she did seem distracted when I couldn't remember the Greek word for stamps. She let me struggle a little while, her silence seemed sad. Then when I gave up, she was suddenly adamant that I never give up, perhaps remembering her younger brother who wrapped himself around with the veil of self-destruction.

I must write a memoir about last summer. It was hot, a group of Christian girls on the street lectured me about God, my mother thought I was laughing when I was actually crying, I saw a dead bird being eaten by green flies, and the next day was the fourth of July. Parades of people pushing through the dark, sweating, maximum security (we stood where the Boston bomb was originally to be planted), a couple kissed in front of us, the fireworks were loud and hopeful. But I was hurt on the inside, only smiling to make my mother happy, I wanted to mourn. I wanted to sit beneath that bridge and have the whole city deserted, lights still twinkling, fireworks still booming like thunder above me. I wouldn't cry, I'd just let the dark in. In the dark there is clarity of mind, which is why I write now.

The rain was blowing so hard, the currents, the gray sky, I wanted to run wild and free through the wind so bad. I needed to come up here and write not only about ideas, but to run. I run now, but not hard enough.

Bruising

I did cry, almost
in trying to find where I can spill the blood
so the light slants just right, to make it ruby

Though I live black and blue
night and shore, hushed
for the sand-shift
swells that harbor
the beating pulse
where I love step forth
and I'll drown
full of only

talk to me

talk to me

talk to me

like waves to
pull me up
and gasp
summer breath
I kept my silence
for more

I lived in the cradle
of a thick-carried wound
and it made my sunset just eve

White Wall

*In remembrance of the Smyrnaen poet Demetrios
Capetanakis, who, in the words of John Lehmann, had a
"genius... for giving himself..."*

DIMITRI

I spent the whole day behind my quietly shut door. If
I slam, my father will hear my presence in the echo
and I don't want him to realize I'm still here. So I
open my window to rainy cataract winds, sprawled
on floor with pen and book. But I'm tired of doing
nothing when I have epic music stuck in my head. So
I look through my box of poems and photos, heart
searching, you know? But sometimes I can find just as
much in the white of my wall or the wood of my
desk. Like solid, and strong, because they seem to
hold me still and tell me to breathe, slow down, *slow
down slow down slow down slow down.* You'll crash! He
says, Safonov says. You.Will.Crash. Because the scale
is long and the world beats at a lower pulse than your
own, he says. And my fingers tangle and the music
breaks and the unfinished measures die inside of me.
I told you, he says, I told you you'd crash.

SAFONOV

When he plays, it's like waves or wings arching
forward. Sweeping like an electric storm past entire
dark fields. Louder, louder, so loud that half the notes
are wrong. But he plays with such conviction and is
so believing in himself in the most beautiful way. Last
night's lesson, I could not find the words I wanted to
say. So we sat in silence and then I swallowed and

asked him what he wanted to be. Then he turned and drew a sharp breath like he'd just felt pain, so I quickly followed up, "Your music was powerful." But these are Dimitri's last lessons and I worry about him. "What do you think you'll do in college?" He shrugs his shoulders. "You know, it's not easy being a pianist," I say.

"You too? *You too?*" He's breathing hard like he's suffocated and knocks down the bench as he rushes out the door. The silence of the white soundproofed walls starts to hurt my ears. I call for him, and almost want to cry for him because I deeply wish that I had never said anything, I wish that I had told him he could play anything, I wish that he could walk back into the room and forgive me now and play for me.

FELIX

Yesterday George came to my garage and asked me to remove the piano from his house. Why? I asked. Doesn't Dimitri play that piano? But George would not listen or respond.

The hour before she died, my mother had called and told me she wasn't feeling well, so I got into my car and drove immediately. I remember catching a glimpse of two people hugging in an empty field and feeling like I wanted to cry in front of someone. When my mother didn't answer the door, the light was golden enough so that it was entrancing and I was so exhausted and upset. Children were shouting and laughing in the playground nearby. I remember thinking how strange it was to be able to hear a crowd but see only silent things like trees and rows of houses.

"Why are you just sitting there?" he asked.

"Because nobody's answering the door."

He knocked on the door, and knocked harder.

"She's gone, George."

"You idiot. She just called me."

"She called me too. She must have known."

He began to kick down the door.

I tried to calm him. I told him that I'd bring my tools and take down the door quietly, but he wouldn't listen. George never listens to anyone when he's holding back tears because he's so focused on keeping it together. And because I know this about him, I try to be there for him whenever I can.

As we're loading the piano onto the truck, I catch Dimitri staring at us from the balcony. He burns on the inside, just like his father. I try to wave, but he's already turned back to go inside.

That feeling of being too late for her, my mother, and my customers who don't rely on my help anymore, and that feeling of wanting to cry in front of someone. I could not bring myself to turn on the engine and drive past empty fields and light. The silence behind the door I cannot break.

MARY

It's not right to not water the pots when it's dark and night and cold. Flowers are only as red as they can be when you water their hearts all year round. But mama doesn't let me water the pots because they're on the balcony and the balcony is full of ice. *Don't we still have souls in the winter?* For now though she can't hear me because she's sleeping under white sheets. But the kid upstairs is awake, awake because he opens the balcony door then shuts it quietly, then opens again, like he doesn't know if he wants to step in or out. He thinks no one can hear him, I can hear him. Open, shut, open, shut like tick tock tick tock then stop, then I stop because my hands slip and the hose falls to make a wet mess so that I fall and slip then *crash* like loud cracks, but there were no china-glass pieces to run on the floor so the sound did not carry. I see it. Below, below his white coming red like blood. And there is no sound because no one saw. Only I heard the door shut last. It's coming dark dark because the sun's red and there is no sound so that I'm scared to breathe hard. And the water still runs from the hose but it's slowing with the dark because the dark is cold and it gets to ice so that it freezes on the inside. No water no water no soul no summer. But I don't call mama because mama doesn't like wet messes. Right now she's sleeping under white sheets.

GEORGE

The woman downstairs turns away when she sees me and holds her daughter close. When we meet face to face she backs up against the wall and turns white. *Are you so afraid of me?* She takes out her key and scrambles to get inside her apartment. I'm not a killer, just the father of a crazy killing son. "Dimitri's not crazy," she whispers. *So you think he fell off the balcony on purpose?* You think there was an actual reason? Just last week he knocked down a whole drawer of china for no reason. He said he was trying to find something behind the cabinet. Dimitri, I ask, what is it you're looking for? Tell me, what could be behind the cabinet? *I know you want to speak, stop this burning on the inside and tell him that you love him and hold him close.* It can't be so hard, speak up Dimitri, speak up, I shout, stand up for yourself. But as soon as he started with Safonov, he got quieter and quieter, and he won't ever look at me. Look me in the eye, I scream. But it's like he's searching the wall behind me. *What are you searching for?* What are you looking for? And I hear my voice like a broken echo because Dimitri won't listen or respond, quietly shut, and I feel so embarrassed. And I know that because Dimitri fell, he too will be embarrassed to live with that open brokenness and I know that he will never speak to me again.

SAFONOV

He won't open his eyes to me. I know you better than anyone, Dimitri. You have opened your heart to me. With the very first note of your Prelude, you sang me your song. Open your eyes. And through bloodied and bandaged coverings I can make out wild swan eyes. Two dark dead beads. The living glint was that flame, his burning fire.

"You." He says. "You betrayed me."

I know you tried to kill yourself. You always played the downbeat a little too hard. You always played the beginning like it was the end.

"Why did you do it?" I ask.

But I know why.

"You know, music is omnipresent—that's what makes it so beautiful," I say.

The dark settles in and half-shadows him. Are you still with me? Stay with me.

I grasp his hand but he whimpers like the dying honk of a swan. His fingers long and white, they could always reach way more than an octave.

"You are not broken, Dimitri. Listen to me. You are not broken. Do you hear?"

He turns his head slowly, like a ghost awakening. I do not cry for him. Because if I do, he'll burn out like water poured on fire. He'll think his strength is not strength but weakness because I'm crying. It *is* strength though. *Channel it Dimitri, channel it into something good, into the music of your life.*

So I leave with a hard pain in my head, watch his slim body on the metal rack of a bed. Summer will come soon, and the nights will be shorter, the sun out longer, burning. I close the door, slip out, leave him behind. He thinks I'm a traitor. And I cry because it must be my fault. It must be my fault. You. He said. You betrayed me. *Oh Dimitri, let this be our last lesson.*

DIMITRI

You are   awake awake   open   shut   open
shut then stop   Broken
then *slow* then crash *down*   It   carries   far
inside of me   the music dies inside of me   You
Are   dark dark, only I   I   heard
the door shut last   Broken
              to breathe hard not to break like china glass
so the sound did not carry   Slow   your bones
bones broke   soft and white and long
Broke   Down   Listen to me
was powerful   Listen to me
am I a swan   *You are* a ghost they say   *Not*
white and falling *Broken*   it   hurts   downbeat
          You   You betrayed me   louder louder
so loud   Breaking   Have I?   Because

I gave it all, I cannot find what to bring it back. What I
spent in falling was the music I had lost. With nothing
left to give, I gave myself. What I spent in falling was
blood running down my forehead. But now I am here
and it's all contained in white bandages that I cannot
break. She tells me that my strength is coming back.
I'm not empty because my bones are coming back
together, not broken anymore.

33

Congregation

White gowned priests shook
too much incense
into every
corner with a
bless you,
I could not breathe

Upon that pile of bone
the dog was staring
silent, Black eagles nested
pinned half dead
they'd eat me if I died

To run, I ran to the
lake, Deer scattered
like I would eat them.
As I sat by the water
they came
looming, waiting

I did not run, I let
them crowd around
me and the lake
And we lived together

Mrs. Barbara

Mrs. Barbara opens the door before we even knock.

"Oh, my darlings! You've grown so tall!"

She's aged ten years in two. The uncombed wisps of hair, the flimsy nightgown that draws curtain to waning-crescent knees, and large eyes like pools of black—little drops splash their shimmering rims like spearheads and crosses.

"Oh children... God bless them," she breathes into sobs, "I'm sorry, I cry for everything these days. Even when the clouds cover the sun or sometimes it's cold outside... " Her voice trails on, a slow unraveling from the spool. Into a pile of loose string, her knees give way.

Agathi leads her mother to the couch whispering, "Her brother died a month ago."

Mrs. Barbara sighs, "What can I say? What can I do? I guess life flies by before you know it."

She leans on my shoulder and dabs her face incessantly with a floral tissue, drying tears that have not been shed.

I Have Come to Write

It is because I did not know how to stroke his hair or how to even speak to him that I have come to write.

Before he goes to sleep, my brother stretches and pulls at his pillow to chase away the dreams that leave him in tears. The other night, he ran to my bedside screaming my name. The house kept silent and his scream died into me as he lay his head on my shoulder, *what happens when we die?* He used to rub the smoothness of my nails when he was little, and did so now. I think my silence scared him. The silence of no answer to the loudness of his screams, as if he were small, and lonely, as if he didn't matter. So I told him of a valley full of dandelions and a herd of goats grazing in that valley surrounded by blue misty mountains and the sun peeking in between. Then he turned to me, the full of the moonlight in his eye, "in my dream I saw God." When he finally fell asleep, I fell too. In circles of darkness that I'm not afraid of anymore. My mother woke me and took me to her bed so I could find my sleep again. She stroked his black hair. I turned and saw the moon, double-sized, and gasped down a whisper of "oh God."

When we visit my grandmother in the summer, some nights she sings songs from her childhood and my brother sleeps to them. When my grandmother falls asleep, the memory of her own mother's song carries through the music into dreams, then into quiet sobs that wake me. It's not like my brother who dreams, then screams awake. My grandmother cries through her sleep and the pain is long and dulling and self-inflicted. It's like breathing too fast and being tired because of it, rather than being tired and therefore breathing too fast. My grandmother can hear my hard woken breath though. She turns to me: *go to sleep.*

Sleep and I'll tell you later. Once as we were walking home from the beach, she sighed. If I hadn't been so close to her, the sound of her breath would be only a passing summer breeze. She worries to death. She worries when I go. She worries when we're on the plane. I do not remember what my grandmother told me when I left that summer, though she did grasp my hand. Whether she was turning away or looking me straight in the eye, I would not know. But shouldn't I know if she looked me in the eye? *Sleep and I'll tell you later.*

I have come because my little brother asked me about death. And because I did not know what to say, and because I'm older, and because I felt like I had to speak, speak and say *sleep, we'll talk about this later.*

That's why I write. For questions that hurt my heart enough to let sob wail in it and choke my throat from the bottom up. I want him to know that love is what saves us from ourselves. I wanted to tell him to love. My grandmother loves. She loves everyone and even cries when strangers die. Or it must be that others' death reminds us of our own, so that the more we feel about our own deaths, the more we'll cry for the death of others, death itself. I know because I am afraid.

I have come because I feel myself slowly pulling away, like I'm resisting my own blood because it's rank and looks dangerous. Words did not seem sufficient in those circles of dark, that quiet summer breeze. My grandmother turned away, I turned away. After that, all I could do was listen. The world has been drifting from me, in snow spells and white hibernations. Soundless shapes. I needed something I could not say or point to or even imagine. When the snow fell, I would stop to listen and I could hear nothing nothing nothing. And the gray was around my bruise into the sky and I was maroon sobbing on the inside.

I have come to write to my own silence, the tears that were supposed to be words. I wanted to tell him a story, but could not look her in the eye. All I could do was write.

Light and Shadow

Light and shadow simmered quietly beneath the hot thick air.
And I worked to a thin boil, my younger brother's tears
condensing mid-sphere, the curtains blew in, breathing summer
breath. He swelled at the very end—like when the nurse was
cutting his nails he closed his eyes and shed a tear.

"I love you" he whispered. She kept cutting with her long
white fingers. He swelled to the very fullest like a droplet
on the edge of its cliff.

My brother will condense midsphere
he turns and dreams but loses all in sweat
for light and shadow simmer quietly near

He closed his eyes, he shed a tear
the curtains blew in breathing summer breath
my brother will condense midsphere

Swelling as the end comes near to near
a droplet's fullest on its falling edge
light and shadow simmer verging here
to tear and burn like time like skin that peels
blooming in reverse to bloom to death
my younger, younger brother

As to the nurse he said *I love you dear* then
light and shadow moved so quietly near
the lines between them are no longer clear

Because the sun's about to disappear
it's strange she keeps to stir that boiling broth
she should know he'll soon condense midsphere
for light and shadow simmer quietly near

Car Wash

We had to roll up the windows, not to drown in water and sound.

The manager told my mother to let go of the wheel and brakes. But as the conveyor belt eased us onto the winding, she grasped the wheel again in shock. Then the manager turned abruptly to repeat, "It's time for you to let go." In moments like these when the world moves slow—conveyor belts, afternoons like falling leaves—we hold onto images, phrases, like prayers and memories before going to sleep. I recited the manager's phrase, *it's time for you to let go,* over and over.

It's a strange irony to be holding onto the phrase *let go.* Chained to something that wanted me to be free, I found myself torn during my piano performance. I could not stop myself to breathe, living uncontrollably and wild on the desperate impulses of my being. Playing music is like drowning. Though you are fighting to breathe, you just want the passions of the currents to overtake you. Last week, three hundred twenty five students were on board a sinking ship from South Korea. The Ferry Sewol. So many drowned. So many passions, so many lines clung.

One boy's final moments were recovered from a video on his phone. His father decided to share it with the world. But by doing so he killed the personal memory of his son. Otto Frank did the same with Anne. He gave her words to the rest of the world so she could live on through the beating pulse of a widespread remembrance. But on the way, he lost her as his only Anne, his daughter only. When I shared my Blumenfeld piece, I lost the dark passion I used to hold—passion raw, and screaming, and bright. Now my passion is rehearsed. Park Jong-dae had his son's face blurred and covered in that video. Otto oversaw the production of millions of Anne Frank's diaries. Passions once and again.

The car wash ended much sooner than I'd imagined. When they told us to step out, I stepped out reluctantly. Sometimes I think I prolong my driving lessons just so I can hold on to the slow-rocked reverie that comes from being a passenger on board. Three men cleaned the interior of our car, the ferry Sewol was washed, empty and replete, with salt water. Our air freshener was 'ocean breeze' and its scent made me feel like my performance would go wrong because it was artificial and would eat away at the wholeness I had gathered from the quiet streams running down my window at the end of the conveyor belt. To counter 'ocean breeze' I tried to relive how far and deep I swam last summer.

To remember solitude is to remember how it was only the wind, the water, the intense light.

The day of the car wash was full of intense light. So was the chapel I played in. I fully remembered my solitude, my self. Nevertheless, the judges rejected me. And because I did not know how to handle that rejection—to have my whole, giving self, thrown but still remembered—and because I did not know how to handle that confusion, not knowing where and why I went wrong, I let myself into streams of lights. Streams of light that carry over currents and waves

and passions, the three hundred twenty five sparkles
that clear my window so I can look out to the wind,
the water, the intense light.

Hysterica passio

What I did lose, is something I cannot explain
four boys shot in the throat
how I wished so many wishes
how the world smiles without passion
how a little girl tried to catch a firefly
but killed it instead,
believing the firefly loved her
since it did not leave her palm to fly away

I close my eyes in selfish pain for
the verse on hiding and storms
the rotting moth beneath my desk
the shells I've collected,
so hurting and precious they feel like
bones

I picked the dandelion,
I did not catch its wisps in the wind but forced
my wishes to fly into the sunset,
wimp and raw,
like half-corpses
they'll die bynight
I've cried without tears

Someone told me that those who overcome
fear
have real depth
my fear is
real depth

When you look at the photo
of someone who died
It will be how it will be when they
listen to those black boxes,
listen listen listen
because that's where
they are refrigerated
in railway wagons,

burnt coal
take them to
the smoke mines
where four boys playing on a
beach
evaporate

> The video of the bombing was on mute,
> because it was preceded by a pampers ad, a
> baby and lullaby music, calm in a moon
> seed, the baby screaming in a hospital with
> a bloody leg

the music teacher with a cool hand
stops the rush of a passion
that an all out silence now claims
with a listen listen listen
surge, my mother as a little girl would
plead, *tell me more of the story of our lost nation*
and my great grandmother
would look somewhere
beyond

To where I walk the shell-shocked beach,
collecting fragments from the froth,
banded tulips, bruised nassas, cut-ribbed
arks, rusty doves
Bittersweet clams, colorful moons,
baby's ears and angel wings

They lie in my black box
like many unanswered prayers
adding stacks to the smoke of what silence claims

2/15/15 Sunday, 6:31 pm

I can't hold my computer close enough for me to
write this with what I feel. I'm faced with the video
now. A black clad hand grips the orange collar of a
man whose neck curve is arched and rimmed with

light and alive. The ocean in the background is white from too many crashing waves. But I am selfish for wanting to write this in any kind of way. He was so stunned and afraid and quietly reconciling with fate. I have no other assignment than to write what I feel. And I write for no one, no one other than myself. Looking at my own reflection too long, I feel like I'm murdering. I could never press play. My teacher is bleeding. My brother threw up. In the woods, the only thing loud enough to be heard was an ambulance. I'm guilty, because after this I'll keep living life. Clenching unclenching. Help my world.
My mother calls. And I can't find it in my heart to respond in any way.

"O, how this mother swells up toward my heart!
Hysterica passio, down, thou climbing sorrow!
Thy element's below. — Where is this daughter?
(Shakespeare)"

Elli Nicolaidi

There is not much that I do now. So I spend my nights making paper boats. I let silence speak for me, it speaks better anyway. I know that as a fact. When there is silence, I feel the impact of my footsteps ring so darkly within the chambers of my ears. I feel my heartbeat sway to the rush of the blood it pumps. And I learn, and I have learned to feel, not listen. It helps me understand more things… and eases some of my pain.

Before I sleep I make paper boats. One for my sister Chrysanthi, one for my brother Andreas, one for my mother, one for my father. Andreas taught me how to make them. He learned it at school from one of his friends. One morning he asked me to come with him to the shore. He made a paper boat then placed it in the water. It went for a few inches, and then followed the beat of the waves. He was very proud, so to make him happy I asked him to teach me. I still remember how to make them, and I make many. Before I go to sleep I make paper boats. One for my sister Chrysanthi, one for my brother Andreas, one for my mother, one for my father. They ride to the beat of my dreams every night.

But all I hear is silence. Even when I see his mouth screaming, his eyes wide in fear. All I can do is stand there, watch my brother get torn apart. It hurts my heart, tears it open. I can't hold back. I jolt up from my bed and scream. This time I hear it. I hear his scream in mine. I feel a fluttering in my chest flying to the beat of the seconds of the clock.

The clock, the clock, the clock... its hands know no sympathy. They leave the ones that are too slow and never come back for them. His first foot was already on deck, second foot mid-air. *My* hand was already reaching out to help him get in the boat. I remember when he caught my hand, how relieved he looked. Then they grabbed him. His disguise to the ground, his head to the sea. They left the body to leak blood. All he needed was one more second. But no, the clock can't even give mercy to a twelve year old boy.

As soon as I wake up from nightmares, I can't slip back into sleep. It is way too dark... so dark that I can't see my hands and that scares me. I wait and wait peacefully for morning to arrive.

I had opened the door of the cabin to let in some air. The captain of the boat gave us a separate room since Chrysanthi was sick.

"Chrysanthi, it will be good for you. I know it makes you feel cold, but you need fresh air and moonlight," I said.

"Elli, they told you not to come near me."

"Then where will I go?" Tears started to fall but I held them in, for her sake, "Chrysanthi, we're almost in Athens. We'll have fun there together as soon as you get better. Athens is the big city."

It felt so strange to talk to her like this. Whenever we talked, we fought so much. I was sure she was jealous of my blue eyes—they say the true Greeks have blue eyes. My father would get mad at us, "Sisters shouldn't fight like that," he always said.

I stroked her head over and over. She closed her eyes and started to sleep, I let her rest. Something light and feathery tickled my fingers. I lifted my hand to the moonlight and saw a little black moth. It shuddered at the light and flew to the moon. I smiled; my mother once told me, in one of those years before she died, "Moths are the spirits of the dead coming for a visit."

"Chrysanthi, a moth flew past, who do you think it is? Maybe it's father or Andreas… "

There was no reply.

I reached for her hand and held on tightly. Her cold skin a relief to my sweaty palm. I kissed her forehead and left for the deck. Peacefully, waiting my turn.

At sunset, it is the worst. That is why I sleep so early, to avoid its red glare. A red glare like a ripple of blood on blue water. And I remember and remember the color of the sea. The three of us running, gasping, screaming, crying, dressed like old ladies, praying they would shed some mercy on us. Arms, heads, legs, all thrown to sea, it was completely red. The Turks had set all the houses on fire, everything was burning. I heard someone shriek behind us.

"Father!" I screamed.

"Don't worry, it wasn't him," Chrysanthi screamed over the screams around us.

"No! No! It was!" I tried to run to the back of the line, but Andreas was pulling me back and the crowd trying to get in the boat was running me over.

I know it was him. He had that same scream. Once, when I was little, I was helping him in our jewelry shop. He had this special evil-eye necklace. It was not on sale, just there to block the bad spirits. Someone grabbed it and started to run and he yelped like he was on fire. I got scared and started to cry. That is how I remember his scream. I remember it because it made me cry.

And as the boat was pulling away, I looked back, but it was all smoke.

When we arrived, I was alone. It was raining so hard. They put all the refugees together in a building. I looked out the window, narrow streets, big buildings, people rushing. I cried. It was nothing like home, nothing like Smyrna. Smyrna, with its fruitful mandarin trees and sunny shores.

A few years later I married Loukas. We had five children, the first died before we could name him. Then we had Stelios, Andreas, George, and Iphigenia. The worst of our years was when my eldest, Stelios, was sick with the Dengue. Loukas took him outside to play ball—he wanted Stelios to prove he was a man by showing that the sickness didn't bother him. Instead, the ball hit my boy's head and the right side of his body got paralyzed. He still is paralyzed.

"You don't love me anymore, do you?" Loukas asked me after the accident.

"It's your fault... " I left for the kitchen, he left for the other woman.

Then Maria came a few months later screaming, "Elli! Elli! He's dead!"

When I saw his broken body under the window, I could not help it, "I love you, I love you," I wailed.

And there were those nights after he died. Sometimes I heard footsteps on the balcony where he used to smoke. From my bed I would turn to the window, but no one was there… one tear for every turn and by the end I was sobbing. "I'm sobbing because I love you," I would hold my sweaty palms together and say this to the ceiling.

Loukas was always so far away. He led me into thinking that I was imagining he loved me. I felt like we were strangers, that if I ran into him, fell into his arms, hid myself in him, his face would be cold and still. And if I wanted to ride on the sea, he'd watch me lovingly from the shore, then I would keep riding and he'd get so far, so far… sometimes I wonder if he'd ever come after me.

The strangest thing though, was that when I saw him I didn't love him as much. Only when he was away I loved him, and dreamed about him. It made me so angry because somehow a part of it all was missing. I just wish I were the last to see him, not that stupid Katina woman, so I could take his pain and make it mine, so I could say for once, "I love you."

I've hid everything that was his The unbearable pain he gives me, the way he tears all my feelings into shreds and ties them back together to form some disturbing sculpture… Loukas the Smyrna of my heart.

My son Stelios thought it was all his fault since he used to fight with his father a lot for leaving us. I tried to tell him that his father committed suicide because he was a drunkard, a man disappointed with his life. But Stelios wouldn't listen. He'd just throw a sack of shoes over his back and leave for the streets to sell them. From the window I could see a mass of children following him, mocking his limp, mocking his lack of a father to support us. But he would keep walking. Stelios, my soul… Times were so bad with the world war and everything that I depended on a boy as old as my brother. It almost makes me laugh today.

Now he's married with two daughters. Elli, the one they named after me, and Eleftheria. He owns many shoe shops and works with his wife, Panayiota. I like her. She is strong and pretty, and hard-working. I gave her gold flowers for the wedding and she put them in a nice vase. Gold flowers, *Chrysanthi*.

My best days now are when Elli and Eleftheria come to visit. We eat ice-cream, go to the theater, feed the pigeons. But at the end of the day we always sit around the fire and I tell them about Smyrna, the catastrophe of Smyrna. And from the way their eyes widen in fear, I can tell they will never forget. If I could write, I would write. I would write for Smyrna so that no one forgets what I remember every day. But I can't write… so I just tell them and hope they will always remember.

There is not much that I do now. So I spend my time making paper boats. One for my sister Chrysanthi, one for my brother Andreas, one for my mother, one for my father, one for Loukas too. So they can all

escape our burning home and glide safely across the
water to the beat of waves.

Credo

He sighed and I turned to the window, thinking about glittering chandeliers and the passions that broke down when I performed, into sweat and shaking knees, wrong notes and an exploding heart. I wish it could have gone the other way—like muscles in a dancer's calf as he leaps higher than ever before, or a singing voice that comes and comes.

In the lecture hall, history words were forming, but I could only think of the passage I had just read, about moving waves of energy sweeping past dawn in surging storms. All of a sudden, I felt a panic, like I didn't know where I was. Cold lights streamed over my head. It was sharp, it was like having slept. I wish I could have lost myself like that during my piano performance.

I try hard to remember the currents that sparkle deeply, rocks under noon's light, exhausted leaves and distances. I tell myself that I must put everything into that first note I play—only then can I entrance my audience through the beauty of the world's purpose.

And I've held onto that conviction so hard. But many of the things that happened this year have shaken me into a feeling of nothingness and believing nothing. Like the German-wings crash, and the death of my mother's friend, and the massacre of Kenyan students. I want to find some way to gather hope. There's a measure in Blumenfeld's Prelude full of cascading notes that fall into each other, and grow and sigh like shimmering curtains that open up. How my great-grandparents hung onto hope and love;

hands held, they looked back onto a Smyrna the Turks had burnt down, a smoke that had stifled younger siblings, the sea was red with blood. And yet my great-grandmother was able to recite poems a week before she died.

I used to believe that I walked for my inner awareness. So that when I'd feel frustrated or confined, all I had to do was remember that I knew about the ponds and shafts of light because I had seen them. But holding onto my inner awareness just isn't enough when it comes to performing my favorite piece of music, or expressing close emotions to the people whom I love most.

The way the clothes fell onto Blumenfeld's shoulders, as though the world were molded to his figure. His gaze somewhere so beyond—not looking towards the viewer, or away, but glinting like the far ocean, near horizon. And that's what I aspired to be—at ease, simply because I believed in my Work, in truth, in goodness, in hope.

Last summer, my brother pulled me outside to show me a valley full of fireflies. The whole family came out to watch. It was quiet, nostalgic, beautiful. I wanted to stay. But as I write this now, I'm more born into it than anything.